WARNING!

"Up there," said Wanda. "Up in the tree. Right at the fork. In a hollow part. There's—there's a *hoard*."

"A *what?*" we all asked.

"A hoard. A treasure hoard." Wanda blushed. "Well, sort of. Look." She put a hand under her sweater and, after glancing around to make sure no one else was watching, she pulled something out.

At first I thought it was just an old flat brown stick, about twelve inches by two, with a hole in one end. Then Wanda turned it over and said, "There was a little pile of stuff and this was laid on top."

We stared at the glittering letters:

8

The Case of the Treetop Treasure

by E.W. Hildick

ILLUSTRATED BY LISL WEIL

AN ARCHWAY PAPERBACK
POCKET BOOKS . NEW YORK

POCKET BOOKS, a Simon & Schuster division of
GULF & WESTERN CORPORATION
1230 Avenue of the Americas, New York, N.Y. 10020

For Julie—the best

Contents

1

A Cry for Help

"Quick! Help us! He'll fall and break his neck!"

"He'll be *killed!*"

The speakers were Marni Williams and Alison Merrick. The two little kids had come bursting into the headquarters of the McGurk Organization.

McGurk glared at them. The rest of us shivered. The two kids had blown into the basement like a gust of the cold October wind itself. Along with the cold, they'd brought in a whole heap of dead leaves that had been gathering on the steps leading down from the yard.

They'd burst in on a full meeting of the Organization: one of McGurk's Saturday-morning specials. Those present, besides Jack P. McGurk, were Wanda Grieg, Willie Sandowsky, Brains Bellingham (our crime-lab expert), and me, Joey Rockaway. And by Saturday-morning special, I mean this:

McGurk had sent around word that this was urgent top-priority business. But when we arrived we found there was no urgent top-priority case to deal with. There was no case of any kind.

"It's just that it's really important to keep in training," McGurk had announced.

"Training?" said Willie, taking a deep sniff through that long nose of his, which that morning had a bluish-red tip.

He sounded as suspicious as Wanda and I looked. Only Brains, the newest member, seemed the least bit eager.

"*Scientific* training, McGurk?" he'd said.

McGurk's green eyes brightened.

"Uh—yeah—you could call it that, Brains. Real scientific training. Sure."

Then he'd told us how he'd been reading a story where the criminal had been caught because of a small piece of evidence stuck in the dried mud on one of his shoes.

"And you know what that was?"

We shook our heads. Not only Brains, but the rest of us were getting interested now.

"A tiny leaf," said McGurk, nodding his red head as he rocked slowly in the chair at the end of the table. "A little tiny leaf. And that one small tiny scrap of a leaf helped the detective to nail the criminal. It *placed* the criminal. Right at the scene of the crime. When he'd sworn he'd been miles away."

At this point, Wanda had said:

"Oh-oh! I think I see what's coming."

And she gave her long blond hair an impatient flick.

McGurk had ignored her. He'd gone right on to explain how the leaf had come from a certain kind of bush that grew only in the area where the dead body had been found.

"So you see how important it is," McGurk had ended. "Being able to identify leaves."

His freckles spread as he smiled around at us. They looked like tiny brown leaves themselves, spreading on the surface of a sunny pond, when something deep down has stirred the water.

Wanda snorted.

"I *knew* it!"

But again McGurk had ignored her. His smile was focused on Brains who was nodding his bristly blond head and blinking wisely behind his glasses.

"Yes, McGurk," he murmured. "A scientific knowledge of trees and plants can be very useful in fighting crime. Soils, too, and types of rock, and—"

"Yeah! Yeah!" McGurk was quick to interrupt. "But one thing at a time, Brains. Let's stay with leaves a while, huh?" He leaned forward and glanced around. "So what I was thinking was this, men. How it would be great training if we—"

Then Wanda had finished it for him.

"—if we all went out in *your* yard, McGurk. And swept up all *your* leaves. And did *your* Saturday chores for you. Like the time you had us looking for clues

4

out there. That was supposed to be fine training, too."

"Yeah!" said Willie. "Bits of junk. Candy wrappers. Some *clues!*"

"It's just a trick," I explained to Brains, who was looking puzzled. "A trick to get us to do his dirty work for him."

"It is *not!*" McGurk had roared. (But his face had started to get red.) "If I wanted you to do my chores, I'd get you to help clean the basement." He pointed to the corners, where the usual basement junk had started to accumulate. Old cartons, empty gas cans, a muddy spade, an old tin funnel—stuff like that. "No. This is really—"

And that's when the two little girls had come bursting in.

Some of us had started to get to our feet. The kids looked really upset. Even McGurk began to look hopeful.

"Hold it!" he said. "Calm down! *Who? Who's* gonna fall and break his neck?"

"June Boyd's kitten," said Alison.

"He's up there now," said Marni.

"We tried saucers of milk."

"Chicken liver, too."

"Only he keeps climbing higher."

"Higher and higher."

Wanda was on her feet again.

"Up where?"

"Tree," said Marni.

"That *big* tree," said Alison.

"Big tree *where?*" said Wanda.

Again McGurk cut in. He looked annoyed.

"Sit down, Officer Grieg. This isn't a detective job." He turned to the two girls, shuffling in the pile of leaves they'd brought in. "Can't you read the notice?" he said, pointing to the still wide-open door. " 'Mysteries Solved,' it says up there.

'Persons Protected,' it says. 'Missing Persons Found.' Nothing about cats up trees. Huh?''

"But, McGurk—"

"So go call the fire department," said McGurk. "Or get one of your brothers to bring it down. And shut the door on your way out. We're busy."

"Wanda?"

The little girls switched their eyes from McGurk.

"Big tree *where?*" said Wanda.

"In the yard in back of the old Thompson house," said Marni.

"That big, enormous tree there. Oh, please, Wanda!"

"I'm on my way," said Wanda.

After all she *was* a tree-climbing expert. And anyway, it was a *real* emergency, better than some old training session.

"Hey—come back!" yelled McGurk. "You, too, Officer Sandowsky! Where d'you think you're going? Hey—Brains! Officer Bellingham! . . . Joey—don't *you* dare—"

By now we were all on our way, and at first I thought McGurk was just going to sit there, stubborn, rocking angrily in the gathering pile of leaves.

7

"We'll *talk* him down!" he boomed. "We'll—we'll practice crowd control!"

He added that last bit just as we reached the Thompson yard.

McGurk was in charge again, all right! But no.

"All right!" he hollered, as he came hurrying after us. "So this *is* police work. We'll figure it's a *suicide* attempt. O.K.? We'll figure this kitten's just lost all his money."

He'd caught up with us by now. He was waving the old tin funnel. He must have snatched it up from the pile of junk. He put it to his lips like it was a bullhorn.

2

The Rescue Operation

Well, that was typical Jack P. McGurk. As soon as he suspects he's losing his grip, he always pulls something like that. He'll dream up some angle that brings us back into line. I mean, that bit about *crowd control*—that was the clincher.

Because there was certainly some crowd there, in the backyard of the old Thompson house. This was one of the few really big houses left in the neighborhood. It had been scheduled for demolition, and all its windows and doors were boarded up and the yards overgrown with weeds.

But now the place was full of activity again, like there was some kind of kids' block party going on. A block party for *little* kids—because that's what most of them were, all clustered around the bottom of the big tree.

And we could tell the kitten was still there—*high* up there—the way everyone was staring up and jumping around and hollering. One little girl kept screaming— one blast every few seconds, regular as a fog horn. Another was kicking the trunk— this huge trunk that you could have cut an archway through big enough for a small car.

Next to her, a couple of little boys were trying to give a leg up to a third, Tony Gallo, but he couldn't even make the first branch. Another kid—little June Boyd— held up a saucer of milk, but she was so nervous that most of it was spilling down her arm.

A crowd, all right. And badly in need of control. I mean there *were* a few older kids, but they didn't seem to be doing much good. Like Sandra Ennis, for instance. Bossing everybody around as usual. Even as we arrived, she started tugging at Tony Gallo.

"Come down, you little dummy! You'll only force it higher." Then she turned to June. "Give *me* that saucer. Before you spill it all. You'll never entice a kitten down with an *empty* saucer. . . . And *you* get down, too!" she yelled, at an older boy, Tom Camuty, who'd just started testing the stubby bark—stubby with old knots and stumps where someone, hundreds of years ago, must have cut off the branches near the bottom.

Tom looked like he was going to give Sandra an argument, but just then his foot slipped on the stub he was testing, and he changed his mind. Probably he realized *he'd* never make it to the first firm branch, either. It was about ten feet above his head—and he didn't want to make a fool of himself.

In fact his face lit up when he saw us pushing our way through—and that was unusual, because he isn't one of the McGurk Organization's biggest fans. Not by a long shot.

"Hey! Here comes the McJerk Organization!" he said. "Let's see how *they* make out."

McGurk ignored the crack.

"Wanda," he said quietly. "Think you can make it?"

He was glancing doubtfully at those first fifteen feet of rough bark, and the few flimsy toeholds.

Wanda looked up at the tree, taking everything in like the true expert she is. She studied it carefully. Quite a few minutes passed and the crowd was beginning to get quieter. I mean, that really was one big tree, the biggest in the whole neighborhood. It was some kind of evergreen, with needley leaves and bunches of small orange cones swaying up there in the breeze. The foliage itself wasn't thick, but there were so many branches. Many of them drooped down, like a willow's, and they formed a kind of screen to the main trunk. Or the *two* main trunks, because, about fifteen feet up, this great thick branch went out at a right angle above our heads, then turned up at a right angle again, like it was another tree.

The kitten's cries seemed to be coming

from the main part of the tree, though—
very high up.

"Wanda?" said McGurk, anxious now.

Wanda flicked her hair back.

"No problem," she said.

And with that, she started climbing, and
the little kids started cheering, and some
of the older ones started jeering, and
McGurk started his crowd control.

"All right, all right!" he boomed, with
the funnel to his lips. *"Stand back there!
Keep it clear there! Come on, come on!
Move it!"*

The funnel must have done it. Even Sandra Ennis moved back without protesting.
Only the members of the Organization re-
mained near the trunk.

Still with the funnel to his lips, McGurk
turned and nearly deafened me.

"Officer Rockaway," he boomed, *"you
got your notebook?"* Wincing, I nodded.
"O.K. So start taking all their names. Witnesses. In case the subject takes a dive
before Officer Grieg gets to him."

June Boyd started to cry again.

The crowd began pressing closer.

Wanda had reached the main fork, where
the big limb went off at a right angle.

"Back! Stand back!" boomed McGurk.
"Officer Bellingham—you comfort the relative." He gave Brains a shove toward June Boyd. Then he turned to Willie. "Reverend Sandowsky, you get—"

"Huh?" Willie looked startled. *"Reverend* Sandowsky?"

"Yeah. You're gonna be the minister. There's always a minister goes up and tries to talk to the subject. When Wanda reaches the kitten, I want you to—" He stopped. He stared up. "Hey, Officer Grieg! What's the trouble? You got stuck already?"

Wanda was still at the fork, staring down at something, like she'd found a nest. She gave a little start.

"Uh—no. . . . No. I'm O.K."

She peered up through the drooping branches.

"Well, get moving then!" bellowed McGurk.

Willie plucked McGurk's sleeve.

"Hey. Listen. *I'm* no climber, McGurk. Why doncha let Brains be the minister? Or Joey? They *look* like ministers, those glasses they wear."

I pretended not to hear. I began to scribble faster than ever in my notebook. I

15

mean, I had a lot of work to do, all those names and other details. Here's only the *first* page:

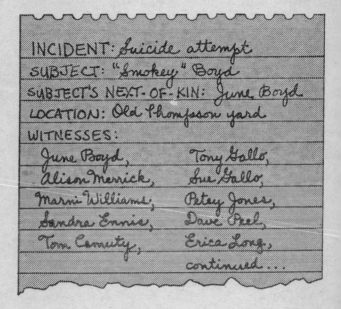

INCIDENT: *Suicide attempt*
SUBJECT: *"Smokey" Boyd*
SUBJECT'S NEXT-OF-KIN: *June Boyd*
LOCATION: *Old Thompson yard*
WITNESSES:

June Boyd,	*Tony Gallo,*
Alison Merrick,	*Sue Gallo,*
Marni Williams,	*Petey Jones,*
Sandra Ennis,	*Dave Peel,*
Tom Comuty,	*Erica Long,*
	continued . . .

Wanda was nearly out of sight now. McGurk put the funnel to his lips.

"When you reach him, Officer Grieg, don't make any sudden grab. Try *talking* him down. Tell him everything'll be O.K.

Tell him he's got all his life before him. Tell him his—uh—his *mother's* here. . . ." He patted June's shoulder. "Also the minister. . . ." He tried to pat Willie's shoulder, but Willie backed away. "Tell him the minister's gonna come up and—"

"McGurk, shut *up!*" Wanda's voice came hissing down. It was not loud but full of fury, and it cut right through the bellowing. "You're scaring him up higher and higher with that thing."

McGurk grunted.

"Huh! O.K." He turned to the crowd. "Hear that, everybody? Perfect silence!"

Well, it wasn't perfect—but there was already a hush created by Wanda's last words. We couldn't see much of her at all, now. Just a leg here and an arm there, and a glimpse of her face now and then, and the red blur of her sweater—slowly moving higher and higher.

Then there was no more movement. A kind of sigh went up from the crowd. June began to whimper. Sandra Ennis shushed her sharply. A twig cracked as Willie moved farther away from McGurk.

Then the needles and cones began to move jerkily at the spot where we'd last seen Wanda, and then we saw her foot, and next her knees, and then the sweater, and then her whole body again as she reached the main fork.

"Where's the kitten?" someone murmured.

"She has it under her sweater, I think," Brains answered. "Yes. . . ."

But now that she was so near safety again, Wanda paused, crouching, at the fork, with her back to us. I saw her fumble about under her sweater and guessed Brains had been right.

Then she straightened up, and, stepping lightly but confidently on those few jutting stumps on the last fifteen feet of the trunk, she came down to earth again.

"There you go!" she said, hauling out the miaowing furry gray bundle from under her sweater and handing it to June Boyd. "Just part of the McGurk Organization's service."

Most of the kids cheered. Even some of the older ones managed to raise a mutter of congratulations.

Only McGurk looked miffed. I guess *he'd* wanted to say something like that about the Organization. So instead he got all snooty.

"Well, come on, Officer Grieg," he said. "You did a good job up there, but crime's a twenty-four hour business. Maybe we've had a *real* case while we've been fooling around here."

Wanda didn't explode, the way I expected her to. No. Instead, she simply nodded, fingering the scratches around her neck. Then she took a last lingering look at the fork in the tree, and hurried out of the yard—even faster than McGurk.

"Hey! What's with *you?*" asked McGurk, as we caught up with her, out on the street. "You want us to give you a *medal* or something? You—"

"No," she said, *still* not looking mad. "Listen, McGurk. All of you. I think we do have a case."

"Huh?"

"Up there. Up in the tree. Right at the fork. In a hollow part. There's—there's a *hoard*."

"A *what?*"

"A hoard. A treasure hoard." Wanda blushed. "Well, sort of. Look." She put a hand under her sweater and, after glancing around to make sure no one else was watching, she pulled something out.

At first I thought it was just an old flat

brown stick, about twelve inches by two, with a hole in one end. Then Wanda turned it over and said, "There was a little pile of stuff and this was laid on top."

We stared at the glittering letters:

3

The Stash

"What else was in the pile?" McGurk asked. He glanced around. "And put that back under your sweater. Don't let anyone else see it until we've investigated some more."

Wanda did as he ordered.

"Well," she said, as we continued on our way back to headquarters, trudging through leaves, "I didn't have much time to see *everything*. But there *was* a necklace—"

"Diamond?"

McGurk had stopped dead. Willie bumped into him. Brains adjusted his glasses, staring keenly at Wanda.

Wanda frowned.

"Sort of. I guess. I'm not sure. I just saw a bit of it. Sparkling."

"Go on!" said McGurk, eagerly, almost greedily. "What else?"

We began to move on again.

"Well—a couple of what looked like ashtrays. At least two—"

"Silver?"

"No. Just ordinary ones—I think. . . . And that's about all I had time to see. I mean there could easily have been more. It's quite a deep little hollow."

"Wow!" said Willie, grabbing McGurk's arm. "Let's go back and get them. There may be a reward."

McGurk looked tempted. Then he shook his head.

"No. Not now. Not while all those kids are still around. We have to proceed carefully on this one, men. It looks more and more like a stash to me. A *burglar's* stash."

"Yeah," said Willie. "That's what I was thinking. Loot. With a reward."

Wanda sniffed.

"Well—I don't know. . . . It's a pretty tough climb. I'm not sure a burglar would want to go to all that trouble—"

"*Sure* he would!" McGurk's eyes were sparkling. Like emeralds. "*Sure* it's a burglar! The very fact that it *is* such a tough climb makes it the best possible hiding place. And burglars are usually expert climbers themselves, remember."

"Yeah," said Willie. "If you weren't a detective, Wanda, I bet you'd make a pretty good cat burglar yourself."

"Oh yeah?"

Wanda started to clench her fists. Willie backed off.

"Sorry!" he said. "I wasn't saying you weren't honest, Wanda—"

"You better not, buddy!"

McGurk stepped between them.

"Cut it out! This is serious. I say it just has to be a regular burglar. And now that we know his hiding place, we've got a good chance of nailing him."

"I agree," said Brains. "I'd like to take a closer look at that notice. And some of the other stuff. Maybe we can trace the owners. As well as pick up a few clues about the burglar himself."

"Right!" said McGurk. "And you'll get your chance, Brains, don't worry. But later. When it's quiet again in that yard."

"You mean you want me to go up there again?" said Wanda.

"Yes. But this time with a bag. Then you can bring it all down for closer examination."

"That's right," said Brains. "Forensic examination. Scientific and thorough. I'll soon know if that's a real diamond necklace."

Now *his* eyes were sparkling. Like sapphires.

"And be sure to wear gloves," McGurk said to Wanda. "We've got our fingerprints all over that notice, I know. But with the rest of the stuff we'll be more careful. Understood?"

Wanda nodded. She was beginning to look pleased at the idea of a return climb.

"Just be sure you don't handle the things too roughly even wearing gloves," said Brains, blinking anxiously. "We don't want to rub off any of the burglar's prints."

Then McGurk's face became very solemn. His eyes got sort of round and less sparkly, and his freckles seemed to move back to give them more space. He put a hand on Wanda's shoulder.

"And Wanda—Officer Grieg—you go into the yard on your own, next time. When it's deserted." He patted her shoulder firmly. "We'll be around—don't worry. But only you will be going in. We don't want to arouse attention."

"Especially the burglar's attention," said Brains.

"Hey!" gasped Willie. "Yeah! Him! What if he's there already? Crouching over his loot. In the shadows. When Wanda climbs up again."

Wanda gulped.

"Yes. I—uh—I mean you won't be *too* far away, fellas?"

McGurk glared at Willie. Then he slowly grinned as he turned back to Wanda.

"Don't worry, Officer Grieg. You'll only have to whistle and the back-up squad will be in there like a flash."

I was just going to say: "Yes. *In* there like a flash, maybe. In the yard. But how about *up* there? Up the tree? I mean, none of *us* is what you'd call a climbing expert."

But I kept quiet.

The whole thing was getting too interesting and I didn't want to scare Wanda off completely.

How I would have felt if there *had* been a dangerous criminal up that tree in the late afternoon dusk, gloating over his loot, and anything *had* happened to Wanda—well, I hate to think about it.

But there was no need to worry.

While we hung around in a vacant lot next to the Thompson backyard, peering through a convenient gap in the tall hedge, Wanda went bravely on with her mission.

And there was no whistle. No muffled scream. No sound of a struggle. Wanda was back in five minutes, with a bulging plastic bag and flushed cheeks.

And in another five minutes we were back at headquarters, with the things laid out on the table, and I was making a careful list.

This list:

CONTENTS OF STASH FOUND IN TREE
IN THOMPSON YARD

DISCOVERING OFFICER: Wanda Grieg
* One BEWARE sign.
* One diamond (?) necklace.
* One diamond (?) ring.
* One ashtray, enamel, with burn marks + inscription: "Holiday Inn."
* One ashtray, green glass, badly chipped.
* One amber (?) cigarette holder, broken in two pieces.
* One pack "Pop Drops" candy (unopened).

"Some *burglar!*" said Brains.

He hadn't even bothered to take his microscope out of its case.

"You *sure* those aren't diamonds?" said McGurk, pointing at the necklace.

"Positive!" said Brains. "You don't need a powerful lens to tell that, either. You got a hammer around here? I'll show you. One little tap and I'll show you powdered glass."

Brains went to the pile of junk—the regular basement junk in the corner—presumably to find something heavy enough to carry out his experiment.

"No! No!" McGurk nearly dragged him back to the table. "But couldn't they be *semi*precious stones, Brains? Huh?"

"And look at the *ring,*" said Wanda, before Brains could say anything. She held it up in her gloved hand, held it lightly between two soft woolly fingers. "See how it bends. And I'm not even squeezing hard." She tossed it back onto the table, where it fell with a dull *chink*. "Right out of a cereal box!"

I nodded. I felt sorry for McGurk. He really wanted that hoard to be valuable. But the truth is the truth.

"Kid stuff," I said. "Obviously."

And I pointed at the candy.

That was when McGurk rallied. His face twisted into a kind of triumphant jeer. His eyes suddenly gleamed again, rather than glistened.

"Oh yeah? Well, what kid would leave it up there, *unopened?*" he said. "You tell me that, Officer Rockaway. Kids who swipe candy *eat* it, not hoard it. Right? Huh? Strange kind of *kid!*"

Wanda sighed.

"Yes," she said. "I have to admit it. It's all very strange."

"Could—could it be a bird?" asked Willie. "Some kinds do steal glittery things. Don't they?"

Brains nodded thoughtfully.

"Magpies . . . yeah." Then he clucked his tongue with impatience. "But things *that* heavy?" he said, pointing to the notice and the glass ashtray. He shook his head. *"Never* magpies!"

"Well, a squirrel, then?" said Willie. "They hoard stuff. Everyone knows that."

"Yeah—nuts," said Brains. "You think these look like *nuts, Willie?*"

"Well maybe a *crazy* squirrel," persisted Willie. "In fact . . ." He bent closer to the table and sniffed. "I do get a kind of animal-y smell from this."

"That so?"

McGurk looked up hopefully. He has great faith in Willie's nose.

But I shot that one down. Give McGurk half a chance and he'll see monsters in everything.

"Why *shouldn't* it smell of animals? Squirrels, even? Regular *sane* squirrels?

Probably one ran over it up in the tree. Or slept on it.''

Then McGurk thumped the table, making us jump and the necklace, the ring, the ashtrays, and the other stuff rattle and dance.

"Magpies? Squirrels? *Dummies!* This has got to be the work of a *human*. And whether it's a kid or a grown-up, something pretty weird is going on." His voice quieted down. "So I'll tell you what we'll do. First thing tomorrow, when it's light, Wanda will put it all back where she found it. Then we'll stake out the Thompson yard. All day, if necessary. See who goes in—and what they do when they get there.''

4

The Stake-Out

Well, I'll tell you right now exactly who or what went into that yard, that Sunday. Also exactly *when*.

McGurk was very firm about the time element.

"We may have to give evidence about this—uh—person's movements. We may need to shoot down any phoney alibis. Check your watches, men."

So we checked our watches against

Brains's Super-Special Astronaut Wrist Chronometer, which gives the exact time for several zones throughout the world. Willie threw us for a while by setting his old Mickey Mouse watch to Moscow time. But in the end we were all ticking away together, ready for the stakeout.

And the result of all this fussing and fine-tuning?

I have the list here:

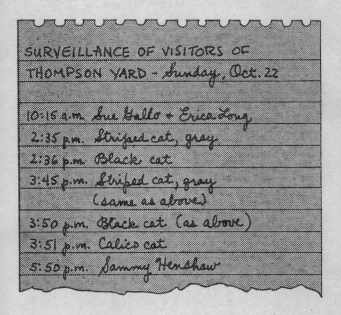

SURVEILLANCE OF VISITORS OF
THOMPSON YARD – Sunday, Oct. 22

10:15 a.m. Sue Gallo + Erica Long
2:35 p.m. Striped cat, gray
2:36 p.m. Black cat
3:45 p.m. Striped cat, gray
            (same as above)
3:50 p.m. Black cat (as above)
3:51 p.m. Calico cat
5:50 p.m. Sammy Henshaw

The cats you can forget. The only one

that even went near the tree was the striped one, on his second visit. He sharpened his claws on the bark. In fact the only reason I recorded the cats at all was to break the monotony. It sure was one long, cold, boring day!

What made us stick with it, then?

Well, maybe the question should be: *Who* made us stick with it? And the answer to that would be McGurk, of course.

But at first it was enthusiasm, because when those two girls went in, we thought we might have gotten lucky. I mean, all right, there was no way either of them could have climbed that tree. But there were other possibilities, which McGurk was quick to point out as we kept watch, crouching in the long grass.

"This could be a meet," he whispered. "So stay down and we'll see who joins them."

I figured he meant some older kids.

But no. For about ten minutes, all those little girls did was look around under the tree, where the grass had been flattened by the crowd.

"They're looking for something," Brains whispered.

"Yeah!" said McGurk. "Maybe looking

for something to *throw* up there, into the hollow. Maybe *that's* the way the rest of the stuff got there. Maybe it's some kind of game!''

Well, those kids *were* looking for something, sure enough. They found it almost as soon as McGurk was through whispering. But it was only a green and yellow striped wool glove that Erica must have lost during yesterday's excitement. And they did *not* toss it up into the hollow.

No. They just went off squealing with joy over having found what they were looking for.

"Anyway," said Wanda, "it would take a star basketball player to throw things that high, so accurately."

"So maybe that's who we're looking for," muttered McGurk.

"Yeah!" said Willie. "A *mad* basketball player! Seven feet tall!"

Willie wasn't joking. But we all picked up on it right away, and the next hour or so passed pretty quickly as we ribbed McGurk and Willie.

"I'd say he'd be undersized," said Brains. "Only about five feet ten. Smoking too much had stopped his growing. That's why he's mad. Angry-mad as well as

35

crazy-mad. So he tosses up his ashtrays and cigarette holder to try and put temptation out of his reach."

"I'd say he was overweight, too," I said. "A *fat*, mad, undersized basketball player. Getting rid of his last box of candy. Putting *that* temptation out of his reach."

"How about the ring and the necklace?" asked Brains, later. "How do we account for *them?*"

"Easy!" said Wanda. "His girl friend returned them to him. Said she was through with him because he was such a lousy player. So we're looking for a *broken-hearted,* fat, mad, undersized basketball player."

"Shut up!" said McGurk, at last. "Whoever it is, he won't come near the place if he hears all this dumb yacking."

During the afternoon, even McGurk began to get bored. We were taking it in shifts by that time. I was with McGurk; Willie with Brains; and Wanda had volunteered to do a spell on her own.

But all that any of us had to report was the cats, and it was only at the very end of the afternoon, when we were all together again, that Sammy Henshaw showed.

And that was no big deal, either. Because Sammy is not a boy and not a man. Just a beagle.

He did stir up a little excitement for a moment or two there, I must admit. This was on account of our remembering Sammy's bad habit of stealing things. Balls,

socks, shoes, walking sticks, old throw rugs—anything left lying around. He even used to hoard the things he'd swiped, too.

"Now if dogs could climb trees," McGurk said sadly, "well, that would be that. Case closed."

"Maybe Sammy's *learned* to climb trees," said Willie. "I mean—well—in the circus on television last week, there was this dog who could climb a whole stack of boxes and—no?"

McGurk's look was withering.

"All right, Wanda," he said. "It's getting dark enough. Just climb up and see if the stuff's still there, the way it was this morning."

Brains clucked.

"Why wouldn't it be? When we've been watching all day?"

"*Some* of us have been watching. But not all day. And *some* of us have been too busy thinking up stupid jokes. So check it out, Officer Grieg. The perpetrator may have slipped in while Joey and I were off duty."

But Wanda reported that everything was just as she'd left it, and by now it was getting quite dark. So we went home, cold and disappointed, and just as baffled as ever.

Maybe if we'd known that certain parts of our joking had come pretty close to the truth, we might have been more cheerful. But we didn't.

The next day was Monday, a school day. Most of us were beginning to lose interest. Only McGurk and Wanda were really enthusiastic: McGurk because he *was* McGurk, and could never rest with an unsolved mystery on his mind; and Wanda because the case involved a tree, and a difficult climb.

So when McGurk called a meeting for Monday afternoon, right after school, and said we'd go through the same routine as on Sunday afternoon, only Wanda was really interested.

The rest of us just hung around by the gap in the hedge, grumbling about wasting our time, while she went in and climbed the tree.

"There's a whole lot of things I could be doing," Brains muttered. *"Useful* things, like fixing up a computer circuit."

"Yeah!" said Willie, shivering. "And I think I got a cold coming. All this hanging around."

"And I could be doing my homework," I said. "I—

Then we forgot about computer circuits, colds, and homework, as Wanda stepped through the hedge and rejoined us.

Her face was flushed.

"He—he's been here again!" she whispered. "Look!"

And from under her sweater she pulled out two more items: both of them shiny and new-looking.

One was a ballpoint pen refill, still in its plastic slot, stuck on a card.

And the other was a small stapler with a bright red handle.

"What position were they in?" asked McGurk.

I couldn't see what he was getting at, but Wanda did.

"Neatly placed on top of the other stuff," she said. "Except that the BE-WARE sign was then placed on top of *them*. Nobody tossed these things up there. They were *taken* up and *put* there."

5

A Breakthrough?

"More junk!" said Brains, a half hour later, as he tossed the stapler and the ball-point pen refill onto the table in our headquarters.

He'd just got back from the crime lab. The crime lab is really his room back home, and for this important stage of the investigation McGurk had wanted us all to go there. But Mrs. Bellingham turned us away. Brains's father was in bed with the flu and the last thing he needed was a bunch of kids tromping up and down the stairs and causing a ruckus in the room next to his. Not even McGurk's most squirmingly polite manner—all whispers and smirks and promises—could shake Mrs. Bellingham's decision.

So we'd had to go back and wait, while Brains conducted his tests alone.

"Junk?" cried McGurk, with a yelp in his voice. (The wait had made him tense up more than usual.) "What d'you mean, junk?"

"This refill for one thing," said Brains. "It's a dud. It's all used up. . . . Mind you, I suspected it when I saw the plastic seal had been broken. Some people do that, you know."

"Do *what?*"

"Stick the old refill into the card after they've fitted the new one in the pen. *Then* they throw it away—the old refill and the card together. I've done it myself."

"Go on," groaned McGurk. "So what about the stapler?"

"Busted. Useless. A write-off. Look." Brains picked up the stapler and broke it open. "No spring. It must have fallen off when they tried to get this end staple un-jammed. A cheap foreign brand.''

McGurk glared.

"What we expected is a *crime* report, Officer Bellingham, not a *consumer* report. What else did you find? What's this, for instance? This red smear on the ballpoint pen card?''

It looked a pinkish orange to me—just a faded ink stain on the back of the card.

Brains shrugged.

"I don't know. I—''

"You *don't know?* You? The lab expert?''

Brains blushed.

"Well, I didn't think it was important. I mean it certainly isn't *blood*, if that's what you have in mind. I—I could take a scraping and—''

"Don't bother!'' The remark came from an unexpected quarter. Willie. He was bending closer to the card. "That's tomato juice. I can smell it from here.''

"Thank goodness *someone's* on the ball!'' jeered McGurk. "Good work, Officer Sandowsky!''

"Well, it's still junk, anyway,'' said Brains, blinking angrily. He picked up the

card and sniffed. *"I* don't smell any tomato juice."

"That's because you don't have Willie's
nose," said McGurk. "And—hey!—why
aren't you wearing your gloves? You're
putting your own prints all over it."

This time Brains smirked.

"Doesn't matter. If you'd waited for my
full report you'd know that."

"Huh?"

"There *were* no prints. Not on this, and

not on this. That was the first thing I tested for. Both objects had been wiped clean. And I do mean *wiped*. Not accidentally smudged."

Some of his old respect for Brains had returned to McGurk's expression.

"You *sure?*"

"Positive. Not a ridge, not a whorl. Not a *trace* of a fingerprint."

McGurk frowned and began slowly rocking in his chair.

Wanda was frowning, too.

"But it's only junk," she murmured. "I mean, why would anyone bother to wipe his fingerprints off *junk?*"

"That's what I'm trying to figure out!" muttered McGurk.

"Somebody playing tricks?" I suggested.

"Obviously," said McGurk. "But why? What's the *point?*" He looked up at Wanda. "Was that candy still unopened, Wanda?"

"Yes. You still think if it wasn't for it—?"

"It could be just a kid's game. Yeah, yeah!"

McGurk was rocking rapidly now. He squeezed his eyes shut.

"Maybe we should open it ourselves," said Brains. "See if it really is candy."

"Yeah!" said Willie. "We could—heh! heh!—scientifically test it. In our mouths."

Brains gave him a scornful look.

"What? And maybe drop dead, foaming at the lips?"

Willie gulped, his grin fading.

Brains turned to McGurk.

"Maybe *that's* the point, McGurk. Maybe the guy's a nut. A homicidal maniac. Maybe he *wants* some dumb kid to find the hoard, and try out the candy, and get poisoned. Why don't you have Wanda bring it down and let me test it *really* scientifically?"

"A nut, yes," murmured McGurk. "But somehow I don't think he's *that* kind of nut. I mean, why would he go to all the bother? He'd just leave the candy lying around on the ground someplace. . . . No."

"I think the person's a miser," said Wanda. "A kid, maybe. Maybe a grown-up. But someone who can't resist even junk, so long as it glitters. After all, a miser *would* polish it up—that kind of miser. Just to gloat over its shininess. That could explain the prints being wiped off."

McGurk nodded.

46

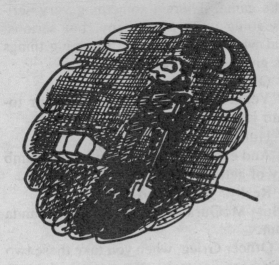

"Yeah," he said, slowing down his rocking, "yeah. . . ." Then he stopped. "But why hoard it up in the tree? Why not in his house? Or a hole in the ground, in a box?"

None of us could give him an answer to that.

Then a faint crooked smile came to McGurk's face, and his eyes gleamed, and he smacked his left fist into the palm of his right hand.

"It's a genuine *mystery*. It is *not* just a

kid's game. There's something very serious going on here. Creepy, but serious. And what you said about glittering things has given me an idea, Wanda."

"Oh?"

"Yeah. You too, Willie, with your tomato juice."

"Huh?"

"And even you, Brains, with your dumb way of getting rid of used refills."

"Really? I don't see—"

But McGurk was addressing Wanda again.

"Officer Grieg, when you take these two items back up into the tree—next, right after this—I want you to bring down that BEWARE sign. I don't think we examined it closely enough. I have a hunch that it might just give us the breakthrough we need."

6
The Sign

"Now," said McGurk, when Wanda had returned and the BEWARE sign had been placed on the table. "Let's see exactly what we do have here."

He looked around.

"Brains," he said, "how about these glittering metal letters? What's your expert opinion?"

Brains pushed his glasses farther up his nose and bent over the sign.

"Well, one thing I can tell you right away. They're *not* metal. They're plastic." He gave the letter *B* a cautious but firm dig with his thumbnail. "Yes," he said. "Definitely plastic. Made to look like chrome."

He eased his thumbnail along the edges of the first *E*.

"And they're stuck on. Some kind of cement. Rather than pressed on like thumbtacks, I mean."

I suddenly remembered something.

"Sure!" I said. "I've seen some just like that in the hardware store. You can buy them separately. 'Make Your Own Sign,' it said."

Wanda nodded.

"Now that you mention it, you can see it's a homemade job by the slight unevenness of the word itself. The *W* is higher than the other letters. Right?"

"Right!" said McGurk. "And the first *E*'s a bit crooked. Whoever did it did a pretty crummy job." His face was flushed now. "Willie? Any views?"

Willie sniffed.

"Yeah. Well. Huh—the wood. That's a good piece of wood. Good tough wood.

I'm not a bad carpenter and you can take it from me. That's a piece of real—"

"—good wood." McGurk finished it for him. "Yeah. But I was thinking more on the lines of your nose than your hobby. How about—"

"—the smell?" This time *Willie* finished it for *McGurk*. He dipped his nose until it nearly touched the letter *A*. "Yeah. I was coming to that." He straightened up. "Smells like at one time it had a light coating of that preserving stuff. That—uh—that *creole* stuff?"

"You mean *creosote?*" said Brains.

Willie nodded vigorously.

"Yeah. That stuff. For yard furniture. Fences. Outdoor stuff."

"Great!" McGurk clapped his hands and kept them squeezed together. He was enjoying this! He was even beginning to get that obnoxious gloating look. "And this hole at the end here, in front of the *B*. Ideas, anyone?"

I was glad Brains was able to tell him— and in such technical detail, too.

"Why, yes." Brains lifted up the sign to get a better look at the hole. "Sure. That's a screw hole. It's been drilled and countersunk."

"Huh?" grunted McGurk, losing some of his bounce. "Counter-what?"

"Countersunk. It's been made wider at the top, so—"

"Yeah," said Willie. "So the screw head fits flush. Didn't you know *that*, McGurk?"

"All right, all right!" snapped McGurk. "So it's a screw hole. So let's cut out the fancy technical terms and say what it *means*, huh? What it *tells* us."

"Well—it was fixed to another piece of wood," said Brains. "You can see the faint marks of it on the back. A crosspiece, vertical, about one-and-a-half inches wide."

We crowded around. Even McGurk hadn't noticed this. And I was so pleased to see McGurk taken by surprise that I made a diagram of the back of the sign right away, showing the faint marks Brains had mentioned.

But McGurk wasn't put down for long. No, sir!

"So?" he said, with a challenging look.

Brains shrugged, but obviously hadn't anything to add right then.

Without giving our crime-lab expert time to think of something, McGurk turned to the rest of us.

"How about the *other* end? Willie? Joey? Wanda?"

"Well, there's no hole *there*," I said, frowning. "But—"

"It's kind of rough," said Wanda. "I can tell you *that!* I've had to be pretty careful not to scratch myself, carrying it up and down the tree under my sweater. It was almost as scratchy as the kitten."

"But it isn't exactly *jagged*," I said, beginning to see what was in McGurk's mind.

Brains snapped his fingers.

"Hey! No! But it *could* have been jagged," he said. "Probably was. Look! See how it's been trimmed at the ragged end.

Clipped with pliers or something. You think—?"

But McGurk wasn't going to let anyone beat him to the final answer.

"I think this is just *part* of a notice," he said triumphantly. "BEWARE OF THE DOG, probably. My guess is that the person who's been stashing things—that person swiped the sign and broke it in half because he thought BEWARE would look good on top of his hoard. . . . No?"

Brains was shaking his head.

"No, McGurk. You heard what Willie said. This is good hard wood. Teak, maybe. And you don't just break that stuff over your knee."

"Well it certainly wasn't *sawed* off!" said McGurk.

"I agree," said Brains. Now he was beginning to act almost as obnoxious as McGurk himself often did. "It *has* been broken. Yes. But not by any pair of human hands."

"Wow!" gasped Willie. "You mean—some kind of *ape?*"

"No, Willie," said Brains. "This has been broken by a *machine*. Look. Look at these scratches, scuff marks, on the letters. See how they get deeper toward the break?

It's a wonder that last *E* wasn't torn off. But then of course if wouldn't have been a sharp impact, would it?" he murmured thoughtfully, more to himself. "No. More of a slow, steady, crushing movement . . . at an angle. . . ." He looked up and around, blinking. "Something very heavy did this. Something *driven* into it, or against it."

"A car?" I said, suddenly excited.

"Or a power mower?" said McGurk, lighting up again. "A power mower at the edge of someone's driveway? Where the sign—?"

"I think Joey's probably right," said Brains, bending closer to the sign again.

"Just hand me that magnifying glass of yours, McGurk. It's rather a poor one compared to mine, but—"

McGurk didn't argue. Eagerly, he handed over the magnifying glass and held his breath with the rest of us, while Brains peered at something just above the final *E*.

"Yes," he said. "A tiny flake of paint. Caught between the letter and the wood. Yellow paint. . . . See it?"

McGurk snatched the glass and stared.

"You're right, Officer Bellingham! Good work!"

"So let's say it was a yellow car. Or a truck. Because power mowers don't usually come in that color and—"

"A yellow whatever!" said McGurk, cutting in triumphantly again. "The point is, it fits! It still fits!"

"Fits what, McGurk?" Wanda asked suspiciously.

"My theory," said McGurk. "Listen. Somebody's sign got broken, right? Probably—no, *certainly*—by accident. Right?"

"Go on," said Brains. "I'll buy that. So?"

"So what do they do with the broken sign? Huh? They toss it in the garbage, of course." McGurk's eyes were shining.

"The way most of the other stuff had been tossed in the garbage."

"I'm not sure I'm with you, McGurk," said Wanda—but more respectfully now.

"Remember the tomato juice on the pen refill card? And the broken stapler? The cigarette holder snapped in half? Not just junk, but garbage! Trash! . . . I'd say this sign and most of the other stuff was picked out of the cans or cartons lined up on the edge of the sidewalk on collection day— Thursday."

"Yes!" I said, getting his drift at last. "So if we find out who was seen foraging around in the cans—"

"If!" said Wanda. Now she was scornful. "Big *if!* . . . I mean, think how many people do that. I've often stopped to take a closer look at a pile of junk myself, if I notice anything interesting."

"Yeah!" drawled McGurk. "But with *this* particular garbage can it's different." He tapped the sign. "If—*when*—when we find out whose sign this was, they may be able to tell us who they saw poking around in their junk. And *that's* why I said this could be the breakthrough!"

We nodded. There are times when you just have to hand it to McGurk. Even

Wanda was looking impressed. Impressed and excited.

"It shouldn't be *too* difficult," said Brains. "Tracing the owner, I mean. There are plenty of dogs in the neighborhood and quite a few BEWARE signs. But this is homemade. Unique. *Somebody* must have seen it before. . . . No?"

He blinked around. None of us was exactly leaping for joy. Even McGurk's enthusiasm was beginning to fade a little.

"That's just it!" he grumbled. "Until something like this crops up, you never really notice the *kind* of sign, how it's *made*. Just what it *says*." Then his eyes brightened. "But at least we know it wasn't on a gate. Or stuck up high on a tree. This was a fairly low-level sign, screwed to a couple of stakes. Right?"

We nodded. We were all thinking hard.

"Come *on!*" pleaded McGurk. "*Some* of you must have seen it. Fairly low down. Near the edge of a driveway. Probably on a lawn—"

"*Very* low down," said Brains. "I'd say no more than a foot from the ground. Low enough for a car's bumper to just clear it."

"Huh?"

"The yellow paint, Willie. From the

body of the car. Bumpers themselves aren't ever—"

"Hold it!"

Wanda was jumping up and down.

"What? Don't say you . . ."

I could tell McGurk hardly dared go on. But he didn't have to. Wanda was nodding her head rapidly, her eyes tight shut.

"I do! I do! I remember it now. Somewhere—somewhere on my way to school. Nearer to the school than my house— but—"

"The address, girl!" McGurk was snapping his fingers. "Where? Where?"

"Well. . . . I'm pretty sure it's a house along Wilson Boulevard—"

"Pretty sure?!" howled McGurk. "I thought you said you remembered it?"

"I did! I do!" Wanda had a quick chew at her bottom lip. "The trouble is . . . well . . . you stop noticing something like that. . . . Its *exact* location. . . . It—it becomes sort of just part of the general background."

"So *think!*" McGurk growled. "Come *on!* That's an order, Officer Grieg. Shut your eyes and *concentrate!*"

But Wanda was shaking her head.

"I have a better idea. Why don't we just

60

follow the route from my house to school. It's *sure* to come back to me then.''

Well, it certainly was a better idea. In fact it was a *great* idea. Because in less than ten minutes we had traced the exact house. I mean, it just had to be: with a brand-new BEWARE OF THE DOG sign nailed to a tree by the gate, and two small bald patches on the lawn at the side of the driveway, about two feet apart.

And when McGurk pointed to the fresh tire tracks cutting up the grass at the edge, near those patches, we could hardly wait to get to the front door and ring the bell.

Dangerous dog or no dangerous dog!

7
The
Accident

As soon as McGurk rang the bell, there
came from somewhere inside the house a
loud barking. It got louder and was accom-
panied by scampering scratchy sounds.

Willie and Brains took a few steps back.

Then there came a tremendous thud
against the door itself, shaking it.

This time, I have to confess, *I* took a
few steps back. But I was in good com-
pany. McGurk was right there at my side.

Only Wanda stood her ground.

"It's O.K.," she said. "I've met this dog before. He's harmless enough."

"He'll bite off all your heads!" came a woman's voice.

But there was a big grin on her face as she opened the door, and Wanda breathed a big sigh.

"It *is* the same dog," she said. "Hi, pal!"

Then the dog made a screechy little whimpering sound, burst past the woman, and flew straight for Wanda's throat. A big shiny black dog. With big flashing white fangs.

"Oh, no!" groaned Willie. "It's one of those killer dogs!"

But it was O.K. The dog had only leaped up to put his front paws, as big as boxing gloves, on Wanda's shoulders, so he could hold her still while he licked her face.

And his ears were floppy.

"Killer-schmiller!" said the woman. "Bruce is a Labrador retriever. You're thinking of a Doberman pinscher, son."

"Yeah, well—the notice," muttered Willie.

"Hah! That's just to deter prowlers, really. And to warn people who might not like their clothes mussed up by an over-friendly dog. Down, Bruce!"

Obediently, the dog climbed down from Wanda's shoulders, then started to give McGurk's shoes a cautious sniffing.

"What can I do for you?" said the woman, staring at the ID card in McGurk's hand. "Not another raffle ticket, I hope?"

She was peering at the card. I could tell at once that she ought to have been wearing glasses. But she had a lot of make-up on, and her long blond hair was very carefully done, so I guessed that she was one of those women who are too fussy about their looks to wear even a fancy pair of glasses and can't wear contact lenses. Then she brought her left hand from behind her back.

She was holding a cigarette in one of the flashiest, longest holders I've ever seen. Green, to match her silk dress.

She puffed at the end of it, as McGurk began to explain.

"Ma'am," he said, taking out the BE-WARE sign from the inside of his windbreaker, "we found this, and we have reason to believe that it's yours."

That "reason to believe" bit, and the stern way he said it, made her jerk her head back a bit.

Then she bent forward, as if to get a closer look at the sign, but this time I could tell it was an act. After all, those letters were big and bright enough.

"Well, yes," she said. "It does look like part of a sign we once had." She took another puff and looked at us, eyes narrowed. "But why the interest? I—we junked it. Got a better one." She nodded toward the tree. "Prettier. Snappier. No law against brightening up your driveway, is there?"

We looked at one another. There was something phony here. Something not quite right about her response. And the woman was definitely nervous. Her puffing was too rapid to be normal.

"No, ma'am," said McGurk. "We were just interested—"

"Say, what *is* that, anyway?" said the woman, suddenly snatching the ID card out of McGurk's other hand and holding it close to her nose. Then: "*Detective* Organization!" she yelped.

Bruce yelped with her. He started to jump up toward the card, but she pushed him down. Which was a good thing, because he looked like he was going to eat it, and that card had taken me a long time to type.

"Well, yes, ma'am. We're hoping this might be a clue—"

"To *what,* for heaven's sake?"

"Well, the case we're working on. It—"

"All right! I think I get it now." The woman looked grim. "You know all about it, don't you? You saw it happen. And now you're going to use it as evidence if I don't pay up."

Again we stared at one another, this time in sheer bewilderment.

"Pay up, ma'am?"

"Yeah! This is blackmail. You know that, don't you? I could have you arrested for this. Kids, these days! Honestly!"

"But, ma'am, we're *detectives!* We're not *crooks!*" McGurk's face had gotten red. He looked as genuinely indignant as he sounded.

Behind him, we growled and grunted our agreement. Even the dog seemed to give a little rumble of protest as he looked up at his owner.

Then the woman sighed, and shook her head as if mad at herself. She smiled.

"Sorry!" she said. "Sorry! Sorry! Sorry!" She took another puff. "I guess it's my guilty conscience."

"Ma'am?"

"Yes." She looked at us carefully, face by face. Then she seemed to make up her mind. "Can you keep a secret?"

"Well, sure, if—" McGurk began.

But the woman didn't wait. She was obviously only too glad to get this business off her chest.

"*I* broke the sign. Backing the car down the driveway last Wednesday. My first driving error in years and I had to make it in the brand-new Olds!"

"Would that be a yellow car?" asked Brains.

She nodded.

"Yes. You've probably seen me in it. Being driven by my husband. His pride and joy." She shuddered and took another puff. "Thank heaven he's away on a business trip. Should be all fixed, good as new, by the time he gets back."

"My mom did the same thing once,"

said Wanda. "She isn't a very good driver either. *She* hit the gatepost."

The woman blinked snappishly.

"Oh, I'm not a *bad* driver! I tell you— it was my first error in years. But I was feeling nervy that morning. I'd just quit smoking and it was making me— *What? What's wrong now?*"

McGurk was acting like *he* needed glasses this time. His head was thrust out toward the woman's cigarette holder. His eyes were like green beads. There was a tight little smile on his face. Very sinister. . . .

"You say you'd just quit smoking, ma'am?"

"Yes," she said. "Cold turkey. Threw all my cigarettes away, all my smoking materials, everything. . . ." She suddenly laughed and waved the cigarette in its holder. "Oh! I see! Yes, well—the accident shook me up so much, I started again. First thing I bought was a pack of cigarettes. Even before the new BEWARE sign. It happens every time I quit. Some crisis or other."

McGurk turned to us. His face was glowing.

"That accounts for the ashtrays and the

broken holder, men.'' He turned to the woman. ''Could you describe them, ma'am? I think we know where they are.''

She did describe them. And we did know.

''But—'' she was looking puzzled as she stubbed out the cigarette—''I don't get it. So do *I* know where they are. They're in the garbage. With the sign—well—with the rest of the sign. I threw them out last Wednesday. I guess they'll be on the town dump by now. So what's the big mystery?''

''Well, as a matter of fact, ma'am, they were obstructed from your garbage can—''

''*Abstracted!*'' I hissed.

''Yeah—like I said. They were *ab*-stracted from the can by a person or persons unknown. Did you see anyone messing around in there on Thursday, ma'am— collection day?''

''Hah! Fat chance! Who stands watch over their *garbage?*''

McGurk sighed.

''Oh, well . . . thank you for your time, ma'am, anyway.''

''You're welcome. And remember: This is a secret. If my husband ever gets to hear—''

''Don't worry, ma'am. So long as it has

nothing to do with the case itself, all information is treated by the McGurk Organization as strictly confidential."

"Well, I should hope so!" But the woman was grinning as she fixed a fresh cigarette in her holder. "Good luck in your investigation, anyway."

"Yuff!" agreed Bruce, as we trudged off.

It was getting dark. So was McGurk's mood.

"If only she *had* spotted someone!"

"Well," I said, "at least we know for sure where some of the stuff came from."

"If it *matters!*" said Brains, just as despondent as McGurk.

Our leader took this as a challenge. Immediately, he got brisk.

"Sure it matters!" he said. "Like I told you before, something very creepy is going on here. And I intend to find out what it is. So tomorrow afternoon, after Wanda's taken this sign back—"

"Tomorrow *afternoon?*" said Wanda.

"Yeah. I mean it's too dark for you to be climbing back with it now." McGurk paused, then his face brightened. "Or is it? Do you think—?"

"No, no." Wanda hurriedly shook her

head. "No. You're right about tonight, McGurk. But I was thinking of getting up early and replacing it before school. I mean, we don't want to alarm the hoarder, do we? Like if he was to go up sometime during the day? He'd see right away that it was missing."

McGurk nodded.

"Good thinking, Officer Grieg!"

"But what if he goes up *tonight?*" said Willie.

Wanda's lip curled.

"Listen! If *I* can't climb that tree in the dark, no one else can. No human, anyway."

"Huh!" grunted Willie.

He didn't sound very convinced.

I think he still had a soft spot for the idea that there was some kind of ape loose in the neighborhood.

8
The Latest Addition

Wanda confirmed her expert opinion the next morning, in the school yard.

"You put it back O.K.?" asked McGurk.

"No problem."

"*Had* anything been disturbed?"

"No. It was just like I'd left it. No ape, Willie. Sorry!"

McGurk got down to business.

"O.K. Well here's what we do today. Something we can do right here in school—and next door." He nodded across to the

Junior High. "We find out who was absent from school yesterday."

"What?!"

Even Brains looked puzzled.

"Sure!" said McGurk. "We're pretty certain it's a kid, right? . . . But to have put those things up in the tree yesterday, it would have to have been done during school hours. So. . . ." He grinned around. "We find out who was absent."

"But if they're in bed with flu—" Willie began.

"Not *all* of them will be," said McGurk. "Some may be just getting over it. Others might be *pretending* to be sick. Others could just be playing hooky. And it's someone like that who's guilty. Got to be!"

"And just *how* do we find out, McGurk?" said Wanda. "Go to the principal's office and demand to check the attendance lists for *every grade?*"

"I think *I* see," I said.

McGurk didn't give me the chance to explain.

"We know who was absent from *our* class yesterday, don't we? And you, Brains—you know who was absent from yours?"

"Sure! You mean—?"

"I mean all we need do is ask one or two kids from every class. They'll tell us who was absent. So we write down the names, and then we'll have a complete list of possibles." He looked at his watch. "We can start now, and go on during morning recess and even at lunch if necessary. O.K.?"

Well, it was a good idea, I guess. But it still took us all of our free time to get those names.

"How many altogether?" asked McGurk, after school, back in our headquarters, when I'd finally combined everyone's list into one neatly typed master list. This one:

June Ellis	Barry Hathaway
Gary Pearson	Ernest Lovat
Burt Rafferty	Jean Lowney
Anne-Marie Jacopli	Sandra Ennis
Teddy Brooks	Melvyn Biddle
Samantha Pabst	Pam West
Patty Hynes	John Devereux
Clark Horwitz	Chris Andrews
Jerry Wild	Dick Magnani
Angie Micheson	Dee-Dee Baker
Stewart Leman	Shirley Rappaport
Stan Whitely	Walt Carmichael
Roger Shanks	Ziggy Baer
Harriet Crosby	Peter Thomas

"Twenty-eight," I said.

"Does that include the names Wanda got?"

"Yes. She gave me her list before she went to check on the tree again."

"Don't forget this, though," said Brains, looking over my shoulder. "Some we can eliminate right off. Like poor Jerry Wild with a broken leg. *He* couldn't even climb the stairs. And—"

That's when Wanda got back.

And that's when all thoughts of absentee lists flew from our heads.

"Hey! What's with *you?*" gasped McGurk.

Wanda was very pale. Two bright spots of red on her cheeks only made the greeny-whiteness of the rest of her face more startling. She was also out of breath, and clutching her stomach.

"I—I—uh—"

"Take it easy," I said, steering a chair behind her, thinking she'd had a fall.

"It's—" She flopped down. Then, "Look!" she said. "Just take a look at this! The—the latest addition!"

She was tugging at something, pulling it from under her coat. Our eyes widened. It was something shiny again—yes. But very different from the rest of the stuff.

"Wow!" gasped Willie.

"Hey!" growled Brains.

"*That* isn't junk!" I said.

"That's *really* loot!" cried McGurk, getting up and leaving his chair rocking wildly.

"You can say *that* again," muttered Brains, carefully taking the article in his gloved hands. It was a small bowl, with fancy handles. "This is solid sterling silver! The best!"

9

Intruders

"Solid *what* silver?" asked Wanda.

"Sterling," murmured Brains.

He still held the bowl upside-down.

"See this small marking stamped here?" he said. "That's the hallmark. That's the official mark they put on gold or silver articles in England. Guarantees that it's genuine."

"Looks like a lion," said McGurk, holding the magnifying glass close. "You sure it isn't just some kind of a trademark?"

"Positive," said Brains. "The initials

stamped here are the *maker's* mark. The lion is the hallmark. This other one with the crown tells you where it was tested. The fancy letter here is the code letter for the year." He looked up. "This is a genuine British antique silver bowl. Probably worth hundreds of dollars."

McGurk didn't argue with *that*. He gazed at the bowl with pure delight. He didn't even object when I took the magnifying glass from him and held it so that Wanda, Willie, and I could get a better look.

Personally, I was a bit doubtful. I mean, for a kid of *his* age—only just turned ten— Brains seems to know a bit too much about *everything*, not just science. I sometimes think he invents some of his information. But I copied those signs down as part of

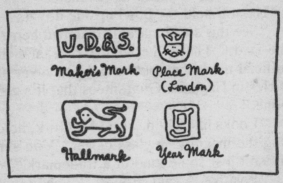

the evidence (and also to check on them later, at the library), and here they are:

By the way, there was really no need to check. Brains was right.

McGurk hadn't doubted him for a moment.

And as soon as he'd taken a second look through the glass, and said, "Yes, you're absolutely right, Brains!"—he made his own assessment.

His own assessment of the *case,* I mean.

"This puts the whole thing on a different level, men. Up until now it's looked like kid stuff. Now it's major league." He placed the bowl carefully in the center of the table. "What's more, I think I now see the *real* motive for putting all that junk up there."

Even Brains couldn't out-think McGurk on that one.

"Oh?"

"Yeah!" said McGurk. "In fact I'm sure of it!" He slapped the table, making the bowl bounce a little and give out a fine melodious ringing note. "The rest of the stuff was a dry run!"

"A what?" said Willie, giving a far from dry sniff.

"You mean—?" I began.

81

But McGurk was all for taking the credit for this himself. Rapidly, he went on:

"Whoever left the stuff in the tree wants that hollow for a *serious* stash—for *real* loot. But he had to see how safe the place was. So he put the junk up there to see whether it would be spotted and disturbed. Right? Right?"

We slowly murmured our agreement.

"Right!" said McGurk. His eyes were shining. "I tell you, men, we're up against a real criminal this time. A really juicy opponent—as cunning as they come!"

"So what do we do now, McGurk?" asked Wanda, her voice hushed with awe. "Take it to the police?"

"What?!" McGurk's pleased expression vanished. "After all the work we've put in?"

"But, McGurk," said Brains, "this is a valuable article. Worth hundreds of dollars."

"I know," said McGurk. "But what happens if we do go to the police? The cops stake out the place and maybe scare the guy off. So then he finds *another* place for the serious loot. Because there'll be more to come now than just this bowl—you can count on it."

"But—"

"But so far *we* haven't scared him off, have we?" McGurk went on. "I mean we've *proved* how successful *we* can be. So I say we should wait at least one more day—see what he brings next."

"Well . . ." Wanda began doubtfully.

"And just to be absolutely sure," said McGurk, *"I'll* stake it out. Personally. Tomorrow. I'll take the day off. I'll fake a stomach ache in the morning."

Willie sniffled again.

"Yeah!" he said. "I think I'll take the day off, too. See if I can shake this bug off out in the fresh air."

McGurk shrugged.

"Anyway, the next thing is to put this bowl back exactly where you found it, Wanda. Now. You can always check again first thing in the morning, ready for me to begin the stakeout."

"You think that's safe?" I asked. "There's still a couple of hours before it gets really dark. Maybe he'll be coming again during that time."

"So what?" said McGurk. "Let him. It'll save me the job tomorrow. I mean, we'll *all* keep careful watch and if he does show this afternoon, we'll know who it is.

Then we can make an arrest."

Wanda looked uneasy at those last words.

"Or tell the police," she said. "And let *them* arrest him. He may be armed and dangerous!"

"Whatever!" said McGurk. "Only let's do it now. If he gets there and finds the bowl missing, *no* one's going to be arresting him."

Well, I don't think any of us expected we'd be surprising someone up that tree during the rest of that afternoon. Not even McGurk, really. And certainly not so soon.

That was why we got such a shock.

I mean there we were, only just that minute arrived at the gap in the hedge, with McGurk telling Wanda to be careful how she went, when we heard them.

Heavy footsteps on the gravel at the side of the old house. The swish of long grass, as the feet left the path. The *clump! clump!* across the shorter grass near the tree. Then the men's voices.

"Yeah! This is the tree. Why doncha just hold the ladder for me while I slip up there?"

"O.K. But take it easy now. The ground's kinda slippery just here. . . ."

We were staring at one another. Willie had been about to risk a peek but McGurk hauled him back, pulling him down into a crouch, and making signs for us to do the same.

"*Stay* down!" he whispered. "Keep your heads down or they'll see us! What we have to do is *crawl* in, through the long grass, until we get behind the bushes to our right. O.K.?"

We nodded, already down on all fours.

"And slowly. Inch by inch. Without making a noise. O.K.?"

Again we nodded. Then McGurk lifted his left hand, listening.

There came a rattling. Then a gruff, "O.K. I've got it steady. Go ahead." Then the creaking stomp of feet on metal rungs.

McGurk must have decided that it was now safe to proceed. With a quick follow-me wave of the hand, he led us through the gap.

10
The Note

McGurk had looked very stern when he'd warned us about not making a noise. But when we finally reached the bushes, and he slowly got to his feet and peered out, he was the one to break our near-silence. He gasped. A loud choking gasp.

"*Look!*" he whispered harshly, as we all began to rise behind him. "*It's a couple of cops!*"

We stared.

One of them was just a pair of dark blue pants, halfway up an aluminum ladder, the top part of him screened by the drooping branches. The other had his back to us as he held the ladder. His hair was whitish-gray.

"Don't tell me we've got a couple of crooked cops on our hands!" whispered McGurk—partly in amazement, partly in disgust, but mainly with eagerness.

"Not Patrolman Cassidy, *surely?*" said Wanda, in a shocked whisper.

The gray-haired one had just turned his head slightly, letting us see his profile. A ripple of the same kind of shock went through the rest of us. Even McGurk seemed to share it.

For it *was* Patrolman Cassidy. The elderly cop who used to come around to schools and talk about road safety. And our special friend.

Why, he had even visited our headquarters during the Case of the Nervous Newsboy! And he had appreciated our efforts so much that he'd rewarded us with a pair of old handcuffs.

They'd been hanging on the wall of our headquarters ever since—our pride and joy. The thought of having to take them down and hand them back to Mr. Cassidy—in a way *using* them on *him*—made me feel sick to my stomach.

McGurk gulped.

"But—what *are* they doing here then?" he whispered. "I mean—"

"Some *loot!*"

The voice had come from up the tree. It was followed by a shower of objects: the BEWARE sign, the stapler, the ballpoint pen refill, the glass necklace. . . .

"No sign of an antique silver bowl then?" said Patrolman Cassidy, plucking the necklace off his shoulder.

"Not unless *this* is one!"

One of the ashtrays fell—the heavy glass one—just missing Patrolman Cassidy's head.

"Hey! Watch it, Morelli!"

The other man was already beginning to climb down. He was carrying the rest of the stuff in his upturned hat. He was a much younger cop, with thick black sideburns and a thin brown face.

"Talk about a bum tip-off!" he grunted, reaching the ground and dumping out the hatful of junk at Patrolman Cassidy's feet.

While the elderly cop stared down at the odds and ends, we turned to one another.

"Tip-off?" whispered Brains. "What *is* this?"

McGurk was breathing heavily and chewing his bottom lip. I could tell he was really baffled for the moment.

"Well," Patrolman Cassidy was saying, "I never did think it amounted to much. Though I don't *know,*" he added, shaking his head, suddenly looking as baffled as McGurk himself.

Wanda sighed.

"Anyway, it isn't *them!*" she whispered. "Obviously."

Glancing back at her, I saw the bulge under her coat. That reminded me.

"Shall we tell them now?" I whispered. "About the bowl?"

McGurk shook his head, still frowning.

"We've got to think, got to do this carefully," he muttered. "We don't want them to get the wrong idea. They might think *we* had something to do with it. . . . No. Let's wait until they've gone. Then we'll put it all back—including the bowl. The way we'd planned."

Brains made one of his impatient clucking noises. I think he was about to give McGurk an argument. *I* certainly was!

But just then Willie sneezed.

Now, all right. Any of the rest of us sneezed, we might have gotten away with it. We might, for instance, have been quick enough to stifle it. And even if it *had* burst out, the sound might not have been *that* startling.

But with *Willie's* nose. . . .

It sounded like a tree being felled—all the branches swishing down and hitting the ground at the same second.

"Hold it!"

The cops had spun around. The young one was already two-thirds of the way toward us. He even had his right hand on the butt of his gun.

"Oh . . . kids!" he muttered, when he reached us. He took his hand away from the gun. "Anyway, what are you doing here? Don't you know—?"

"That's O.K., Morelli," said Patrolman Cassidy. "Friends of mine. As of this moment, anyway. . . ." His grin faded. "Hi, McQuirk! Hi, fellas! . . ." Then, even more seriously: "Hi, young lady!"

He was looking at Wanda curiously.

I thought for a moment he'd spotted the lump under her coat.

"O.K.," he said, turning and leading us

back to the tree. "I want you all to look at
this junk and tell us what you know about
it."

"Well—" Wanda began—but McGurk
hurried to take over.

"It's an investigation we're on, Mr.
Cassidy."

"Is that a fact, now?"

"Yes, sir. You see . . ."

And McGurk went on to tell about
Wanda rescuing the kitten, and finding the

hoard, and how things kept getting added, and how we'd traced the sign. Everything, in fact, except about the silver bowl.

By now I was beginning to feel we'd better level with them about that, too. But then Patrolman Cassidy told us something that made me glad we *had* kept quiet about the bowl.

"So you're working on this yourselves, huh, M'Turk?"

"That's Mc*Gurk,* sir. Yes."

"Any leads?"

"Well—nothing really definite. Yet."

"Because you'd better work fast," said Patrolman Cassidy, suddenly grim again. "Because someone doesn't like you guys. You in particular, honey," he added, staring curiously at Wanda again.

For a moment, I thought he'd been referring to Lieutenant Kaspar. But while it's true we had gotten in the lieutenant's hair from time to time, it was McGurk who was usually the target for Kaspar's anger, not Wanda.

Then it was all made clear.

"Show 'em the note, Morelli."

The other cop pulled out a folded sheet of paper. He unfolded it and held it out.

94

"Go on," he said to McGurk, "take it. It's only a Xerox copy."

As McGurk took it, we crowded around.

Then came another round of gasps—much louder than those we'd let loose behind the bushes.

For here is a copy of that note, which later we were allowed to have for our files:

Just like that. Horribly typed. No signature.

Wanda growled. It was a good loud growl, full of indignation.

"That's a *lie!* Someone's trying to frame me! Someone's playing games, and if you think I—"

"Easy! Take it easy, honey!" Patrolman Cassidy was nodding. "I believe you."

```
Wandaa Grieg is a xxi kleptomaniac. McGurk anfd

the others are covering for her. You will find

the silver bowl she stole from Ms. Anne Phillips in

fork of biggest Tree in back yard of old Thompson

house. Along with the rest of her (their) Loot.
```

"Sure!" muttered McGurk. "Take it easy, Officer Grieg!"

He was gripping her arm—hard.

"Except it isn't such a funny game—"

"Funny? It's *sick!*" growled Wanda, interrupting Patrolman Cassidy. "It's— *ouch!*"

That was McGurk, tightening his grip, as the cop continued:

"I mean this junk—all right—a game. But we've inquired already and Miss Phillips's bowl really *is* missing. So—well— that's something else. An old lady like that. She didn't even know it *was* missing, until she had us look in the high cupboard and check. Doesn't use the silver service much, you see."

We were silent for a while now. Most of us knew Miss Phillips. She is one of the nicest ladies in the neighborhood. Lots of kids used to go to her house—and not just for handouts, either.

You see, Miss Phillips is very old and lives alone. We'd run errands for her and do other little chores. Some kids more than others, of course, depending on how near they lived, and whether they passed her front window regularly, and looked to see if she was beckoning. Even McGurk, who doesn't usually go much for that sort of thing—even he used to keep an eye out when he passed.

Like he once said:

"You never know. Old lady—alone. Some day some crook might decide to take advantage of her, and hold her up, and . . ."

Well, this wasn't as drastic as *that*.

Even so. . . .

"Huh—did she have any ideas who might have swiped it?" McGurk asked.

Mr. Cassidy shook his head sadly.

"Wouldn't give us a single name."

"All we asked for was a list of recent visitors," said his partner.

"But no dice," said Mr. Cassidy. "Says so many kids come visiting she couldn't remember. Says it's probably just been mislaid."

"*Couldn't* remember!" snorted Morelli. "More like *wouldn't*! And I didn't buy the *mislaid* bit, either. She's just covering. Too softhearted!"

"Anyway," said Patrolman Cassidy, "that's why Lieutenant Kaspar told us to follow up this note."

He gave it a look of disgust as he took it from McGurk. Then he folded it and put it in a pocket. He smiled sadly at Wanda.

"I guess you got picked on for being such a good climber, honey." He looked up at the tree. "*I* sure wouldn't like to climb that. Even with the box you've been using to start with."

"Box?"

McGurk's eyes narrowed.

"Yeah. . . . Hah!" The cop gave a short laugh. "Think I hadn't spotted *that*, McGraw?" He pointed to the soft earth, where the junk had fallen. "See. There. And there. The depressions. Oblong object, used several times. What else could it be but a box?"

"Yes, but not for *me!*" Wanda was flushed, but much brighter now, glad to feel she was trusted. "Just watch!"

And she went up to the trunk and started climbing.

Well, in her relief and excitement and eagerness, she must have forgotten all about the bowl. Because she hadn't gotten more than five or six feet up the trunk before the valuable antique came clattering down from under her coat.

Right at the feet of Patrolman Morelli.

His dark eyes lit up.

"Well, well, well! See what I see, Joe? . . .

You kids had better come and have a chat about this with Lieutenant Kaspar. *Without holding anything back, this time!*''

11
Cop Talk

Lieutenant Kaspar was in a good mood—
for him. I mean, he wasn't laughing and
joking. But he wasn't snapping and snarl-
ing, either.

No. He just sat back and listened to
everything we had to tell him. In fact, the
only ones he was a bit abrupt with were
Patrolmen Cassidy and Morelli. They had
gone into his office with us. Patrolman
Morelli was still jubilant at catching us, and

he seemed to look forward to getting us in trouble. Mr. Cassidy was the opposite, anxious to put in a good word for us.

But Lieutenant Kaspar's vivid blue eyes flashed up at them both.

"All right! All right!" he said. "A silver bowl has been recovered. That's all we know so far. Why don't you take it around to Miss Phillips and see if she identifies it. . . . I'll take care of *them*."

By *"them"* he meant us—and the way he said it had the younger cop looking pleased, the old cop shaking his head sadly, and the five of us tightening up, bracing ourselves.

But we needn't have bothered.

He listened carefully. From time to time he nodded. Once or twice he interrupted to ask a question—the sort of mild question meant to make things clearer in his mind, nothing nasty. Only at the very end of our story did he ask one that was at all awkward.

"So why didn't you hand the bowl over to the police right away?"

"Well—uh—" McGurk went red. Then he squared his shoulders and looked Kaspar in the eyes and said: "I take full responsibility for that, Lieutenant. I—uh—I *ordered* the others to keep quiet about it. I—uh—I wanted time to think."

"Hmm!"

Lieutenant Kaspar's face went a shade pinker. He gave McGurk a long hard look. Then he turned to Wanda.

"Do you visit with Miss Phillips often?"

"Yes, but—" Wanda's voice started to wobble—"I didn't take the—the bowl! I—I wouldn't even—*dream* of—"

Then the lieutenant reached out. The hand that usually stabbed a gold-ringed finger at us, fiercely, this time rose and fell slowly, gently, onto Wanda's shoulder.

"Nobody says you *did* take the bowl!" he said softly. Then he growled. "Except the creep who sent us *this!"* And then his finger did make a stabbing movement, toward the original note on his desk. "So just take it—"

The phone rang. He picked it up.

"Yes. Put him on. . . . Cassidy? . . . And she's sure it's hers? . . . You did? . . . And? . . . Uhuh! . . . Yeah. . . . I see. . . . Oh, well, nothing we *can* do, is there?"

He put down the receiver and looked up at Wanda.

"And even if I *was* accusing you, it wouldn't be much use," he said. "That was Patrolman Cassidy, phoning from Miss Phillips's. She's identified the bowl, but she says she's sure it's a—uh—*prank*." He scowled briefly at the note. "And she still won't even name any of the kids who *might* have had access to the silver." He shrugged. "So if the victim refuses to co-operate, there's nothing much we can do.

One of the facts of life in *real* police work, McGurk."

"Yeah, I guess," said McGurk, looking really pleased at this cop-to-cop way Kaspar was treating him. "It's—"

"But *I'm* the victim! *I'm* the one who's being framed—who someone's *trying* to frame!"

Both Kaspar and McGurk looked startled at this interruption.

The lieutenant recovered first.

"I see your point—uh—Miss Grieg. Yes. . . . Would you like to make an official complaint?"

But by now McGurk was himself again.

"No way!" he cried. "Uh—sir. . . . I mean this is *our* affair. *We'll* deal with this." He turned and glared at Wanda. "O.K.—*Officer* Grieg?"

"S-sure!" Wanda whispered.

The lieutenant gave McGurk a keen glance.

"You have an idea who wrote this?"

"No. But we have some good leads. Right, men?"

We nodded—some of us more doubtfully than others.

"Fine!" said Lieutenant Kaspar. "So

maybe when you finally track down the perpetrator, you'll let us know?"

"Sir?"

McGurk looked puzzled. Kaspar looked thoughtful.

"Yes. Prank or no prank. I *could* charge him or her with wasting police time."

McGurk's face broke up in a grin.

"Like you keep saying you'll do to us?"

"Right!" said the lieutenant, looking grim. "Only this time I'll mean what I—huh!" He swallowed. "When *you* waste our time, it's only because you're trying to be helpful. But this—" he wrinkled his nose at the note—"this is different. Whoever sent this has a very nasty streak—and if it's a kid it's a streak that needs checking before it gets worse. A good talking-to from Patrolman Cassidy might help there."

McGurk grinned again. He'd been looking rather indignant at the bit about our "only *trying* to be helpful." But at the mention of Patrolman Cassidy, McGurk's scowl lifted.

"Instead of a talking-to from Mr. Cassidy, Lieutenant—"

He hesitated.

"Yes?"

"How about a bawling-out from *you?*"

For the first time ever, we saw a flicker of a grin cross the lieutenant's face.

"Well—maybe. . . . Though I can't say it has much effect on *some* kids I know." Then he looked very serious again. "But no violence—understand? No taking the law into your own hands!"

McGurk looked shocked.

"Certainly not! That would be police brutality!"

Kaspar shot him a suspicious look, but McGurk was absolutely serious himself.

"O.K.," said the lieutenant. He waved toward the door. "Now beat it. I have some heavy paperwork to catch up on."

McGurk nodded gravely—cop-to-cop again.

"So do we, Lieutenant! . . . Come on, men!"

12
The Bellingham Homemade Human Computer

McGurk hadn't been fooling when he'd spoken of *our* heavy paperwork. I mean, I don't know how heavy Lieutenant Kaspar's was, but I'm sure it wasn't anything like the burden that McGurk dumped on us.

For the rest of that afternoon and all during the following day, he had us busy compiling or revising lists. Once again he had us using every minute of spare time in school—during recesses and breaks, and even in class when he thought he could get away with it.

Poor Wanda, for one, got jumped on by Miss Williamson for "not paying attention." Not paying attention! When she was nearly going cross-eyed sifting through her list of absentees, which she had on her lap under the desk.

"All you need to do about *that* list," McGurk had told her, "is strike out those who came back to school yesterday. None of *them* could have planted the silver bowl."

Well, that might not have been so bad. Only three names had needed crossing off (Patty Hynes, Jean Lowney, and Walt Carmichael). But then Wanda, in her anxiety to track down the perpetrator, had gone on to add names of those who'd *started* to be absent on Tuesday. This list had reached thirty-two names by lunchtime, before Brains pointed out she was wasting her time.

"The new ones might have been available to put the bowl in the tree," he said. "But not the stapler and ballpoint pen refill on Monday. Erase them!"

That's what Wanda had been doing when Miss Williamson had pulled her up. Correcting the list back to its original twenty-eight minus three.

Brains, of course, was enjoying all this. In fact he'd practically taken charge of the whole operation. As the day wore on, even McGurk had begun to get a bit glassy-eyed.

"The list of kids who passed the BE-WARE sign house on Wilson Boulevard!" he groaned. "It's getting out of hand. Thirty-five names *already!* It's so close to school, kids from all over town pass it."

"Yes, but we only need to count the kids from *this* neighborhood," said Brains.

"That's what these *are!*" howled McGurk. "Not including any of us!"

But at least it didn't grow after that. Which was just as well. Because when we met in McGurk's basement after school for the final tally, here's what we had:

List A: Kids who'd been in the Thompson yard when Wanda rescued the kitten: twenty-five names.

List B: Regular visitors to Miss Phillips's—kids we knew who stopped by there at least once a week: nineteen names.

List C: Enemies. (1) Enemies of the

McGurk Organization—kids who were always putting us down or kids who'd wanted to join and been turned down. (2) Enemies of Wanda personally. There weren't many in Part 2, but there had been more than enough in Part 1. This was the list McGurk himself was the most interested in.

"You can't be good cops without making enemies!" he muttered grimly, his eyes going over and over the fifteen names. And since it *was* the most important list, I might as well reproduce it here:

PRIME SUSPECTS: Enemies etc. Ⓒ

Burt Rafferty,	Tom Camuty,
Jerry Pierce,	Sandra Ennis,
Manya Handel,	Andy Carling,
Jane Garland,	Sam Whitaker,
Melvin Biddle,	Chris Andrews
Mary Villiers,	Joe Krupke,
Annette Wilson,	Pam West.
Barry Hathaway,	

Ⓒ

The ringed *C*'s scrawled on it were made by Brains. It was his idea to give each list a letter of the alphabet. At first I thought it was just being fussy. Anway, there were two more.

List D: This was the one that McGurk had grumbled about so much. Kids who passed the BEWARE sign house to and from school. Total: thirty-five names.

List E: Kids who had been absent from school both Monday and Tuesday: twenty-five names. (Though this still included a few cases like Jerry Wild, with the broken leg, who couldn't possibly have done it.)

"So they come out," Brains had said, striking these names briskly with his felt-tip pen, reducing the list to an operative twenty-one.

"O.K.," he said at last, pulling some cards from his pocket. "So now we can start."

"Start what?" said McGurk, looking up, blinking, from List *C*.

"Computerizing," said Brains. "Feeding all these names into the computer and seeing what it tells us."

A look of annoyance rippled across McGurk's face—killing the flicker of hope that had started up at Brains's words.

"*What* computer?"

Brains flushed.

"Well—not the real thing, of course. But kind of on the same principle. Using these cards."

They were slips of very thin card, about four by two inches.

"I cut them up myself," said Brains. "Last night, when I got the idea. Actually I've made too many. I did thirty and we only need half that."

He counted off fifteen: the number of prime suspects. We crowded closer. I saw that on the bottom half of each card he already had another crop of letters: *A D E B*. Each letter was in its own perfect one-inch square, and the order was the same every time. Here's a sample:

"*Adeb?*" said Willie. "What's that mean?"

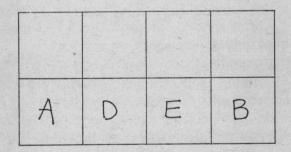

"They're just letters," said Brains. "Each letter checks with one of the lists."

"Except *C*," I pointed out.

"The names on *that* list," said Brains, "are written out in full. One for each card. On the back, like this."

And he turned one of the cards over and neatly printed the name TOM CAMUTY.

"But why in *that* order?" Wanda asked, turning the card back over and pointing to the letters. "Why not alphabetical order: *A-B-D-E*?"

"Because this is the *logical* order: *A-D-E-B*."

McGurk was beginning to look very impatient.

"Go on then! Show us how it works."

"Gladly," said Brains, picking up the Tom Camuty card and pulling a pair of nail scissors from his pocket. "Joey—you take the *A* list. Willie—the *B* list. McGurk—list *D*. Wanda—list *E*. O.K.?"

We nodded.

"Right," said Brains. "This is Tom Camuty's card. Joey, is he on your list?"

"Yes."

"Good." Brains gave the *A* square a little tick.

114

"Willie?" he said. "How about list *B*—visitors to Miss Phillips? Is he there?"

After a long pause, during which McGurk started growling and Willie's sniffling got worse, Willie shook his head.

"No."

"All rightee!" said Brains.

Then he took his scissors and very carefully clipped out the *B* square.

"McGurk! The *D* list?"

"Yeah!" snarled McGurk. "He's on mine all right. But for Pete's sake what *is* this?"

"You'll see," murmured Brains, contentedly ticking the *D* square. "And now your list, Wanda. Is Tom on that one?"

"No," said Wanda.

"Very well!"

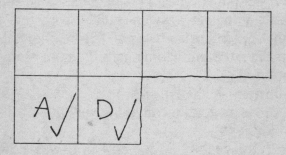

Humming a little tune, Brains carefully clipped out the *E* square.

"So here we have Tom Camuty's card all prepared!"

He put it on one side. It now looked like this:

"Looks like rats have been chewing it!" said Willie, grinning.

"Now we'll do the same for Burt Rafferty's," said Brains, writing that name on the back of the next card. "Joey—"

"Hey! How long is this gonna take?"

We looked up. McGurk was still impatient—obviously. But his eyes had a very bright gleam in them suddenly.

Brains shrugged.

"Five, ten minutes. Maybe longer if you keep interrupting."

"And at the end you're gonna come up with a logical answer, huh? From the— uh—" McGurk grinned. "From the Bellingham Patent Homemade Human Computer."

Brains flushed again.

"It's as good as anything we have available."

"Oh, yeah?" McGurk's grin was now an obnoxious leer. He patted his head.

116

"How about the McGurk Infallible Hunch Machine? Right here."

"You mean you think you *know*—?" Wanda began.

"Not *think*," said McGurk. "I'm certain of it. I suddenly remembered something a few moments ago."

"So?" I said.

McGurk relaxed a little. He nodded at Brains's pile of cards.

"Look, Officer Bellingham—I'm not trying to put you down. You go ahead with your way and we'll see what answer you come up with. If it's the same as mine—great! Maybe we can use the Human Computer sometime when the Hunch Machine runs dry."

"How will we know—?" I began, suspiciously.

"—that I won't cheat?" said McGurk, really hot now. "Because I'm going to write the name down now." He reached out, got hold of my notebook, flipped it open, cupped a freckled hand around it to hide what he was scrawling, then ripped out the page.

He folded it up, put it in his pocket, and stood up.

"While you guys work on the—uh—computer, I'll just slip across to the Thompson yard. I won't be long."

"What for?"

"To see if I can get hold of an extra piece of evidence."

"But I thought you *knew* who it is?" said Brains.

"I do. This is a piece of back-up evidence. Something that will help to *prove* what I already know—and what you'll soon be finding out." He grinned. "*If* that card thing works!"

Then he was gone, leaving us to check through the lists (*I* had to take over McGurk's—who else?), with Brains snipping and ticking and looking very determined to meet the challenge successfully.

13

"War!"

We had just completed the last card when McGurk got back. It had taken us more like twenty minutes. But Brains was still looking very confident—almost as confident as McGurk.

"Well?" I said, as McGurk came in. "Did you find your evidence?"

"I think so," he said. "Did you guys find your name?"

"We're just about to," said Brains.

He was carefully stacking the fifteen

cards into a neat pile, with the names on the underside and the four letters uppermost.

Or what was left of the four letters—because most of the cards had at least one of the squares cut out, and many had two or three missing.

"Right," said Brains. "Here we go. All the *A*'s on top of each other—except where the *A*'s have been cut out. And all the *D*'s and *E*'s and *B*'s too."

Even McGurk was looking interested now.

"Now," said Brains, "we'll take the *B* section first. That's the Miss Phillips's visitors letter. And the reason I take it first is this. It's *certainly* got to be someone who had the opportunity to take the bowl. Right?"

We nodded.

Brains pulled out a small pair of pliers and, with them, gripped the bottom right-hand corner of the pile of cards. Precisely over the *B* square.

Then he lifted the pile, gave it a shake, and a number of cards fluttered out and fell to the floor. These were the cards with the *B* squares missing—cards that weren't in the grip of the pliers.

"Leave them!" he said to Willie. "Those cards are eliminated. The kids whose names are on the back are in the clear."

I nodded. I gave Brains a glance of admiration. I was beginning to see the point.

"Now," said Brains, "we move to the next important letter—*E*." He fixed the pliers so they were gripping the square on the pile of cards remaining. "It isn't as certain as *B* was, but it's *almost* certainly someone who had the chance to plant the stuff while we were in school. Right?"

We nodded. He shook the pile. All the cards with the *E* square missing fluttered to the floor.

Nobody moved to pick them up this time. We all stared, fascinated, as Brains switched the pliers' grip to the next square to the left—*D*. The pile was getting quite thin.

"With *D,* we do have to be careful," Brains said. "It *could* have been someone who usually takes a different route to school. We can't rule that out entirely, can we?"

"Shake the cards!" said McGurk, gruffly.

Brains did, but gently, over the table. Three or four fluttered out.

"We'll probably have to take a second look at *them* later."

"Never mind *them!*" grunted McGurk. "It looks like there's only one left."

"Ah, yes!" said Brains, lifting a hand cautiously and lowering that remaining card to the table, all its squares intact and neatly ticked. "But here again we have to be careful. The perpetrator may have decided to keep out of the way or in hiding while the kitten was being rescued. So—"

"So show it! Turn it over!" said McGurk, his eyes blazing green, his own piece of paper already in his hand. "Now!"

Brains shrugged and, in the same movement, turned the card with the name face up:

```
SANDRA ENNIS
```

Then:

"WAR!" McGurk cried gleefully, and slapped down his own slip of paper:

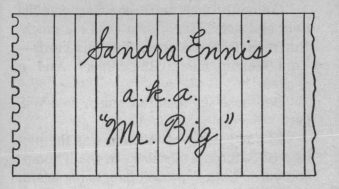

Sandra Ennis
a.k.a.
"Mr. Big"

"Wh-what's *a.k.a.?*" stammered Willie.

" 'Also known as,' " said McGurk, triumphantly. "Remember that's what she called herself the time she kidnapped those dolls in the Deadline Case. 'Mr. Big.' "

Willie nodded and grinned.

"But we made her look pretty small," he said.

"Which is why she waited and worked out this stunt," I said. "Sheer revenge!"

"Yes! Against *me!*" said Wanda. "For being the only girl in the Organization."

McGurk turned to Brains.

"Anyway, how about that, Brains? We checked out—the Hunch Machine and the Human Computer both!"

"But—what gave you the idea, Mc-Gurk?" Wanda asked.

"Going through the Prime Suspects list over and over. It still didn't tell me much. But then Brains started with his cards— Tom Camuty first. Remember? And it clicked."

"But these say Sandra Ennis," said Willie.

"I know! But what clicked was the picture of Saturday morning. In the Thompson yard. Like it was all happening again, with Tom starting to climb the tree." McGurk's face was glowing. "And what I saw was this. I saw Sandra Ennis bossing everybody around. Pulling Tony Gallo away from the tree. Stopping Tommy Camuty from climbing. Telling them they'd only force the kitten up higher. Saying the only way they'd get it down was to entice it with the milk."

McGurk's eyes came back to us.

"Well? Don't *you* see it?"

"See what, McGurk?" asked Willie.

"See what *didn't* happen? That she *didn't* try to stop *Wanda* from climbing? That she *didn't* even raise an objection."

"Wow!" gasped Wanda. "Of course! She—she *wanted* me to climb that tree. She *wanted* me to see that hoard. She *wanted* us to start investigating, hoping

124

that people would see us hanging around there. Me in particular!"

"Yeah!" said McGurk. "A real cunning trap. With the kitten as bait."

"And she must have snuck the kitten up there in the first place!" said Wanda. "Why, it could have been killed!"

"Let's go get her!" growled Willie.

"In a minute," said McGurk. "Joey—get the Xerox copy of the note." He crossed to the door. "We'll take it along with this latest piece of evidence." He opened the door and pulled in a dirty old wooden box. *"This,"* he said, "is what she must have used to stand on. It didn't take me long to find it. I knew she'd keep it handy someplace. In fact," he grinned—"she'd stashed it down the steps leading to the *Thompson* basement."

"But what makes it evidence?" I asked.

"Well, for one thing it fits the marks under the tree that Patrolman Cassidy spotted. And for another, there are footprints on the end where she stood. Uh—sort of."

We stared. They just looked like muddy smears to me. No fancy patterns, standing out clear.

"I don't see—"

"We won't see anything if we stand

around here yacking!" said McGurk. "Come on! Let's pull her in for questioning, before her mother comes home from work."

14
And "War!" Again

Well, we didn't "pull her in" for questioning. Sandra Ennis refused to go one step
beyond her front door. But, as McGurk
said later:

"We got quicker results that way. Did
you notice how she kept looking past us,
scared that her mother might get home
early? That extra pressure was a big help."

At first, however, Sandra was all charm.

"Oh, hi!" she said, opening wide those

big blue eyes and fluttering her lashes. "Have you come to see why I haven't been to school? Well, I'm recovering from flu. I had it very bad and the doctor says I should take an extra week. . . ."

We'd deliberately let her rattle on. But when our silence and accusing stares got through to her, she trailed off. Then her eyes flashed, and her mouth twisted up, and she became her usual bratty self.

"All right, so what *is* this? Another of your dumb games? I heard you've got troubles enough, without bugging other people!"

"Troubles?" said McGurk, softly.

"Yeah! I hear you got a rotten apple in your Organization, McGurk. I—"

She backed away hurriedly. Wanda had taken a step forward, fists clenched. McGurk moved in front of her.

"It's no use, Sandra," he said. "We know all about it. We have the evidence."

He waved us to one side and pointed to the box, which he'd left in the middle of the driveway.

Sandra's eyes flickered. Suddenly she didn't look so sure of herself.

"Evidence?"

"Yeah," said McGurk. "The box you

used to help you climb the tree. When you planted the stuff—including the silver bowl.''

''I—I don't know what you're talking about.''

''Trouble,'' said McGurk. ''That's what.''

''The trouble *you're* in,'' I added.

''You see, that box has a footprint on it,'' said McGurk. ''A beauty. Faint but perfect. Now Brains here doesn't have the equipment to bring it out clearly—but the police do. And when they come around. . . . What's the matter, Sandra? Your feet itching?''

The girl had started twisting one foot behind the other—trying in vain to hide her shoes. Then we *knew* we had her.

"Wh-when they come around?" she whispered. "Here? The—the police?"

"Yes," said McGurk. "It's a serious offense, stealing silver bowls."

"But—but—I—"

"Or wasting police time with dumb tricks, even if it wasn't stealing," said McGurk. "That's what Lieutenant Kaspar told us. Right, men?" He sighed. "So when they come to look at your shoes—"

McGurk flicked his fingers at me—a prearranged signal.

"—they'll also want to check *this* against any typewriter in your house."

By "this" he meant the copy of the note I was holding up.

"The *e*'s aren't in line with the rest," said Brains, pointing out one example with the tip of his pencil. "A little higher. And the tail of the *g*'s doesn't make a strong enough impression. And—oh—there are all sorts of points they'll be able to check against."

"And so prove that you typed it," said McGurk.

"And typed it very *badly*," I added.

"But—I—it—"

"Hey! Why bother with all that fancy stuff?" cried Wanda, suddenly lunging forward and pointing to Sandra's neck, just above the left shoulder. Several scratch marks set close together were just showing over the top of Sandra's sweater. Wanda grabbed it and pulled it down, and there they were, in long lines. "Now it's my turn to shout 'War!', McGurk. Look!"

Wanda tugged at her own sweater and,

sure enough, there on her shoulder and neck was an almost identical set of scratches.

"Where the kitten hung on," she explained. "With me on the way down. With her on the way *up!*"

That did it. Sandra burst into tears.

"But it was only a *joke!* I didn't really mean it to go this far!"

"I *bet* you didn't!" said McGurk, grimly.

"I—please believe me—I just wanted the collection of junk to send you all on a wild goose chase. I knew you'd be curious."

"Junk? *A silver bowl worth hundreds of dollars?*"

"I—that—that just came on the spur of the moment. I—I—"

"Come on, men!" said McGurk, with a look of disgust that was so exaggerated I nearly laughed out loud. "Let's leave the cops to dirty *their* hands with this."

"No! No! Please! I'm sorry! I—"

She broke off, sobbing.

Even Wanda began to look sorry for her.

"Well," said McGurk, "it's no use asking us to conceal a crime. That would make us accessories." He grunted thoughtfully.

"But I'll tell you what I'll do. I'll speak to my buddy, Lieutenant Kaspar, and tell him to go easy with you. On condition—"

"Oh, anything, McGurk, anything!"

"On condition you apologize—"

"Oh, I do! I do! I'm sorry! I truly am!"

"Not to *me*. To your victims."

"V-victims?"

"Yes. To Wanda here, for the mean trick you played on her. To Miss Phillips, for taking advantage of *her*. To June Boyd, for the dangerous stunt you pulled with her kitten. And to Lieutenant Kaspar, for wasting his time."

"Lieutenant—? But—but then he'll *know!*"

"Sure. But if you go to him, and apologize, and come clean about the whole thing, he'll be satisfied. If you don't— well—" McGurk shrugged. "He'll just have to make a regular case of it and send over a couple of patrolmen to bring you in."

Sandra was already pulling on her coat.

"O.K. Sure. Sorry, Wanda! Really!"

And so she fulfilled the first of her conditions and Wanda was very big about it, accepting the apology coolly, but without any gloating.

As for the rest, we know she did what she was ordered because we followed her around. She came out of Miss Phillips's red-faced and weeping, looking very ashamed of herself. I guess that nice old lady had offered her milk and cookies.

She left June Boyd's yard looking a bit mad, and rubbing her shin. Obviously, little June's way of accepting the apology was to kick Sandra good and hard—and who can blame the kid?

But when she left the police department building, her face was neither red with shame, nor angry, nor weepy. It was white and very, very thoughtful. After only ten minutes, at that!

"The lieutenant must have done one of his *extra*-special jobs on her!" murmured Brains.

"Poor girl!" sighed Wanda.

"Poor girl nothing!" snapped McGurk. "Anyway, that's that. Case closed." He looked up at the sky. "There's still a good hour of daylight left. Let's get back to Headquarters and put it to good use."

"*What* good use, McGurk?" Wanda asked, suspiciously.

"The leaf exercise," said McGurk. "A very—"

"Oh no!" cried Wanda, saying it for us all. "We're not going to—"

"Listen! Just *listen!"* said McGurk. "Let me finish. A very *special* leaf exercise. Really."

"How special?"

"Well, when I went to the Thompson yard, I found the box in no time at all," said McGurk. "So, knowing you'd still be working on the computer, I spent another five minutes filling the box."

"Filling it?"

"Yeah! With leaves. All sorts of leaves from trees and bushes in the Thompson yard. Trees and bushes that we don't have in ours. And when I got back I sprinkled them all over our backyard. So *now* the exercise is for us to find as many of those *foreign* leaves as we can."

"Hey, I like that!" said Brains. "I'll get my tree book and we'll label them."

"It'll mean raking up *all* the leaves, of course," said McGurk. "But—"

Wanda grinned.

"O.K., McGurk. You win. But—" she said, turning to Brains, "I bet I find more of the Thompson leaves than you, tree book or no tree book. After all, I *am* the tree expert!"

That McGurk is one great con artist! He even had Willie and me itching to get at those leaves.

All I can say is, it's a good thing he's on the side of law and order. It really is!